Dear Parent:
Your child's love of reading starts here!

Every child learns to read in a different way and at his or her own speed. Some go back and forth between reading levels and read favorite books again and again. Others read through each level in order. You can help your young reader improve and become more confident by encouraging his or her own interests and abilities. From books your child reads with you to the first books he or she reads alone, there are I Can Read Books for every stage of reading:

SHARED READING
Basic language, word repetition, and whimsical illustrations, ideal for sharing with your emergent reader

BEGINNING READING
Short sentences, familiar words, and simple concepts for children eager to read on their own

READING WITH HELP
Engaging stories, longer sentences, and language play for developing readers

3

READING ALONE
Complex plots, challenging vocabulary, and high-interest topics for the independent reader

ADVANCED READING
Short paragraphs, chapters, and exciting themes for the perfect bridge to chapter books

I Can Read Books have introduced children to the joy of reading since 1957. Featuring award-winning authors and illustrators and a fabulous cast of beloved characters, I Can Read Books set the standard for beginning readers.

A lifetime of discovery begins with the magical words **"I Can Read!"**

Visit www.icanread.com for information on enriching your child's reading experience.

For Susan Auerbach,
museum aficionada
—J.O'C.

For Sasha
—R.P.G.

To D.D.—bestest chum
—T.E.

 Printed in the United States of America. For information address HarperCollins Children's Books, a division of HarperCollins Publishers, 1350 Avenue of the Americas, New York, NY 10019. www.harpercollinschildrens.com

Library of Congress Cataloging-in-Publication Data
O'Connor, Jane.
Fancy Nancy at the museum / by Jane O'Connor ; pictures based on the art of Robin Preiss Glasser. — 1st ed.
p. cm. — (I can read! Level 1)
Summary: Although Nancy is excited at the prospect of a fancy class trip to the art museum, the bumpy bus ride to get there leaves her feeling anything but fancy.
ISBN 978-0-06-123607-5 (pbk.) — ISBN 978-0-06-123608-2 (trade bdg.)
[1. Museums—Fiction. 2. Art—Fiction. 3. Buses—Fiction. 4. Teachers—Fiction.] I. Preiss-Glasser, Robin, ill. II. Title.
PZ7.O222Fg 2008 2007018376
[E]—dc22 CIP
AC

1 2 3 4 5 6 7 8 9 10 ❖ First Edition

Fancy Nancy at the Museum

by Jane O'Connor

cover illustration by Robin Preiss Glasser

interior illustrations by Ted Enik

HarperCollinsPublishers

Ooh la la!

I am overjoyed.

(That's a fancy word for very happy.)

Our class is going

to a museum.

I look extra fancy.

So does Ms. Glass.

"I love your shirt,"

I tell her.

Ms. Glass tells us,

"Today we will see masterpieces!

That's a fancy word

for great paintings."

The bus ride is very bumpy.
Bump! Bump! Bump!
Bree is my bus buddy.
"My tummy feels funny,"
she tells me.
Bump! Bump! Bump!

MUSEUM

We stop for lunch.

Bree is not hungry.

But I am.

I eat my lunch.

I eat her lunch too.

I have two eggs,

a juice box,

carrot sticks,

an apple,

and a big cookie.

"*Merci,*" I say.

(That's French for "thank you.")

Now we are back on the bus.

Bump! Bump! Bump!

“We will be there soon,”

says Ms. Glass.

I hope so.

My tummy feels funny now—

very funny.

Maybe two lunches was

one lunch too many.

"Ms. Glass! Ms. Glass!"

I cry.

"I am going to be sick."

"Stop the bus!"
Ms. Glass cries.

The bus stops.
Ms. Glass takes me
to the side of the road.
I get sick.

I drink some water.
I suck on a mint.
My tummy feels better.
But I am not overjoyed
anymore.
I am all dirty.

"I wanted to look extra fancy today,"

I say sadly.

"I understand," Ms. Glass says.

"And I have an idea."

We get to the museum.

"Come with me," says Ms. Glass.

I come out.

Ms. Glass's idea was spectacular.

(That's a fancy word for great.)

"Lucky you," says Bree.

"I wish I got to wear her shirt and hat."

"It is a French hat," I tell her.

"It is a beret."

A man from the museum
takes us to a gallery.
(That's a fancy museum word for room.)

I love all the paintings—
the masterpieces most of all.
We see paintings of trees and lakes.
They are called landscapes.

We see paintings of flowers
and bowls of fruit.
They are called still lifes.

The last painting is a picture of a lady.

"A painting of a person

is called a portrait,"

the man tells us.

"I like her hat and her fan and her beads,"

I tell the man.

"They are lavender.

Lavender is my favorite color."

(That's a fancy word for light purple.)

The man smiles.

"You are a very observant girl."

Then Ms. Glass tells us,

"Observant means noticing things.

Nancy is very observant, indeed."

On the bus trip back,

I do not feel sick.

I feel almost overjoyed.

That night,
I make a painting for Ms. Glass
because she is so nice.

Merci from
NANCY

It is not a masterpiece.

But someday I will paint one.

Fancy Nancy's Fancy Words

These are the fancy words in this book:

Beret—a cap (you say it like this: buh-REY)

Gallery—a room in a museum

Landscape—a painting of nature

Lavender—light purple

Masterpiece—a great painting

Merci—"thank you" in French (you say it like this: mair-SEE)

Observant—noticing things

Overjoyed—very happy

Portrait—a painting of a person

Spectacular—great

Still life—a painting of things such as flowers or fruit